The Summer Night

by Charlotte Zolotow

Pictures by Ben Shecter

An Ursula Nordstrom Book

HARPER & ROW, PUBLISHERS
New York, Evanston, San Francisco, London

For my father
Louis J. Shapiro

The little girl's father took care of her all day. In the evening he bathed her and put her to bed. But the little girl wasn't sleepy.

"I'm thirsty," she said.

He brought her a cup of water.

"I'm hungry," she said.

Her father brought her an apple.

"I'm hot," she said.

Her father opened the window
and the soft night air came in.

She looked out into the darkness.
The sky was full of stars.

The little girl's eyes were bright
as the stars, and her father could
understand why on this soft summer
night she wasn't sleepy.

So he took her up in his arms and carried her down the stairs.

Only one lamp was on in the living room, but the moonlight shone in through the big window, making everything in the room a new shape and size.

The gold clock on the mantelpiece seemed to say,

night-time-night-time-night-time

"Read me a story," the little girl said.

Her father read her a long story in his slow deep voice, but when he closed the book, her eyes were still bright, and he knew she wasn't sleepy yet.

He sat down on the piano bench and the little girl leaned against him and he played some soft nighttime music, so gently the sounds hung like little birds in the air, warm and feathery and sweet.

But when her father finished the song the little girl still wasn't sleepy.

"We'll go for a walk," her father said.

The little girl slipped her hand in his. The screen door closed behind them like a whisper in the night.

Far away a train whistle sounded. The little girl moved closer to her father as they started toward the backyard path. Lightning bugs like little darts of fire led the way.

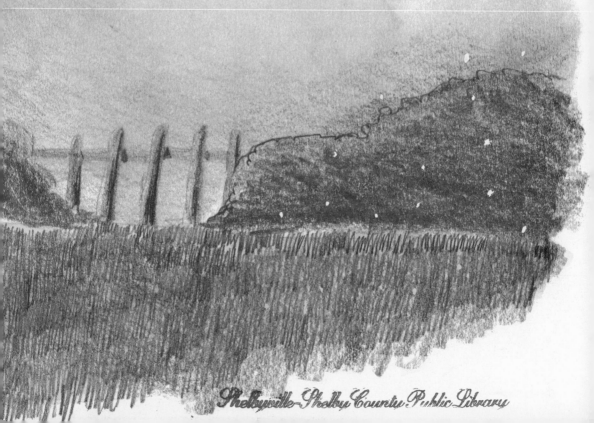

They came to the pond. It looked
like a pool of black shiny ink.

At the water's edge two rabbits
stopped still and stared at them
before they bounded into the bushes
and were gone.

The father and little girl sat by the pond.

On the opposite bank a family of white ducks were sleeping with their heads pillowed in their own soft feathers.

The moon, reflected in the pond, seemed so close the little girl felt she could reach into the water and hold the moon in her hands.

The lilacs from the house smelled sweet and stronger than they did in the daytime.

"Mmmmmmmmmm," said the little girl, leaning against her father.

"Watch," he said.

He threw a pebble into the smooth pond. They watched the circles rippling out and out in the black water while the splash of the stone echoed in the stillness of the night.

"Now, let's go," the father said at last, holding out his hand. The little girl put hers in his and they started back to the house.

The lighted kitchen window shone through the darkness.

Near the house they heard a little bell tinkling. It was the bell their cat wore to warn the birds away.

Whooooooooooo
Whoooooooooooooooooooo
WHOOOOOoooooooooooooooooo
A long sound came from the owl
in the tree behind the house as the
father opened the screen door.

He sat the little girl at the kitchen table and they had warm milk and bread and butter with brown sugar. Now the father saw that the little girl's eyes were dreamy and sleepy at last.

So he carried her upstairs and put
her to bed again. He bent down to
kiss her and the little girl kissed
him back.

Outside the night owl cried again.
Whooooooooo
Whoooooooooooooooooooo
WHOOOOOooooooooooooooooo

But this time the little girl didn't
hear. She was fast asleep.